The Alien Girl

By

Holly Soorty
(Aged Seven)

The Alien Girl: First edition 2020. The events and conversations in this book have been set down to the best of the author's memory, whether that makes them factual is debatable. Some names and details, including Bella's, have been changed to protect the privacy of individuals. Copyright © 2020 by Holly Soorty

All rights reserved. No part of this book may be reproduced by a human or alien in any form by an electronic or mechanical means, including information storage and retrieval systems, without permission in writing from the publisher, except by a reviewer who may quote brief passages in a review.

INTRODUCTION

Hello. My name is Bella Smith, I'm twelve years old, and I have a secret. My mum and dad don't even know it. Before I can tell you my secret, you have to promise me you won't tell anyone. I'm going to have to whisper now, as my parents are downstairs and I don't want them to hear. My secret is I'm half-alien.

CHAPTER ONE

Yummy
(One year earlier)

My mum had just started cleaning her car as I set off to my grandad's house.

'Bye Mum,' I said.

'Bye Bella, and please remember to be careful when crossing the roads,' replied my mum.

'Okay,' I said.

It was the first time I had been allowed to walk to my grandad's house on my own.

I always loved going to my grandad's house. He had so many cool things to play with. He had a toy steam-engine, talking meercats, and a wooden rocking horse. But my favourite of all was his blue telescope.

My grandad knew so much about space, but he had never studied it. He could name planets my science teacher couldn't even name. He knew

more about space than anyone else on the planet.

Twice when I stayed the night at my grandad's house he let me look through his telescope—it was so cool. I could see the moon, stars, and even some planets up close.

I really wanted a telescope of my own, so I could look into space every night.

I asked my dad, 'Please can I have a telescope for my birthday.'

'It's a waste of money. You can already see the moon, stars and Earth with your own eyes. What do you need a telescope for?' Replied my dad.

'I suppose I don't need one,' I answered.

On the way to my grandad's home, I passed the shop 'Yummy'. I had always wanted to go in. All of my friends talked about it. They told me it was out of this world. I didn't understand why my parents wouldn't let me enter. I couldn't even see through the window of the shop, as it had been painted like a starry night.

Oh how I wished I could look inside. I thought to myself, 'the street is empty, I could just take a quick look in. No one would ever know'. I quickly opened the shop door and ran inside.

Yummy was full of alien stuff. There were alien toys, alien sweets and alien spaceships. It was amazing. I now understood why it was called Yummy. This was better than any sweet shop I had ever been in. I wanted everything.

A man with a long grey beard, wearing glasses, started staring at me from behind the counter.

'Are you an alien?' he asked.

I started trembling. I couldn't speak. I was scared. I wondered why he would ask such a thing. The man then walked off into what seemed to be nowhere. I tried to follow him, but suddenly my mum appeared in the shop.

I was confused how she got to 'Yummy' so fast because when I left our house she had just started washing her car.

'I told you not to go into Yummy. You know your father and I don't want you coming here,' said my mum sounding disappointed.

'I'm sorry,' I said.

'You obviously can't be trusted on your own. You will have to come back to the house with me. You can visit your grandad another day when I have the time to accompany you,' my mum replied.

I walked home with my mum in silence.

When we arrived back to our street, I became really confused. It hadn't been my mum washing her car. It had been my neighbour, Fred, washing his car.

Inside our house my mum asked,

'So what did you think of those ridiculous alien things in the shop?'

Before I had time to answer there was a knock at the door. It was the man from the shop.

The man pointed at me and said, 'You stole from my shop'.

'Bella would never steal from Yummy,' my mum replied.

'How do you know?' the man asked.

'It would be impossible. Everything in Yummy belongs to Bella,' my mum said.

The man laughed and quickly ran off.

'Do I actually own everything in Yummy?' I asked my mum.

'Yes darling, you do, but I wasn't supposed to tell you,' my mum answered.

'But I don't understand,' I said.

'You will one day,' my mum replied.

CHAPTER TWO

The Green Creature

At night, tucked up in bed, I heard some rustling coming from the kitchen. I crept downstairs to investigate. Stood rummaging through our fridge was a little green creature with a green antenna. Being only September, I knew it was too early in the year to be one of Santa's elves.

The green creature looked over at me. I was so scared, I ran back upstairs and woke my mum and dad.

'There's a green creature in the kitchen,' I said.

'Stop being silly Bella,' said mum yawning.

I pleaded with her, 'I'm not, there is one'.

'Okay Bella, I will go and take a look downstairs,' grumbled my dad.

'Dad, don't you think you should take something to protect yourself?'

'I think I will be okay,' he said.

Ten minutes later, my dad returned. For some reason he had crumbs all around his face.

'I didn't see anything there, but the last piece of cake does seem to have vanished from the fridge,' he said.

'Dad, there was a green thing. I saw it with my own eyes,' I replied.

'Honey, you must have been having a nightmare. It was probably after visiting Yummy. That is one of the reasons we didn't want you to go there. How about I come and tuck you back into bed,' Mum said.

The next morning, I searched the whole house

for the green creature. I couldn't find it anywhere.

CHAPTER THREE

The Surprise

The next night, I heard some more rustling. This time I went to my parents' bedroom first before going downstairs. I wanted them to see the creature as well.

We all crept down the stairs. The green creature was stood emptying the fridge. My mum screamed. My dad ran upstairs and grabbed his mobile to call the police. I couldn't help but smile.

I heard sirens in the distance. They got louder until there were blue flashing lights shining through our living room window.

A policewoman shouted through a megaphone,

'We believe you have an alien in your house?'

'We did have an alien in our house, but it seems to have vanished,' my mum answered.

I went upstairs and sat watching the police from my bedroom window. Many of our neighbours had joined them, including Fred.

I heard the floor board creak behind me. The green creature suddenly appeared and came over to me.

'Ssshh, don't be afraid. I could never hurt you,' the creature said.

The creature continued, 'Please don't tell them I'm here'.

He sounded much older than I thought he would.

'What are you?' I asked.

'They are right, I am an alien,' he replied.

'Why are you here?' I asked.

He then snapped his fingers and turned into my grandad.

'I am from the planet starland, I am your grandad. I have been disguising myself as a human being since I came to Earth',

'Does dad know?' I asked.

He laughed, 'No. We flew here together 35 years ago, when he was 1. I brought him up as a human. Nobody else knows, well, other than you!'

'What were you doing here last night?' I asked.

'You were supposed to come and visit me yesterday. When you didn't show up, I came to check on you,' Grandad replied.

'You really should get yourself a phone Grandad, then you could have called to check. Anyway, why are you here tonight?'

'I tried the cake in the fridge and it was so delicious. I came for the final piece, but it was gone,' replied Grandad.

'How did you get to Earth?' I asked.

'Your fridge, isn't an ordinary fridge. One day soon I will show you what I mean.' he replied.

'Why did you come to Earth in the first place?' I asked.

'It is a long story, one we don't have time for right now,' answered Grandad.

CHAPTER FOUR

Home

My dad came into my bedroom. My grandad quickly clicked his fingers. This time he turned into a baby alien.

'Please can we keep him?' I asked my dad.

'No, he might be dangerous,' my dad replied.

My dad went off to fetch the police. Before the police arrived, my grandad clicked his fingers and turned back into a human.

'I wanted to show you your dad's reaction to the baby alien. That is why I brought your dad up as a human. If he thinks aliens are dangerous, and he is an alien, everyone else probably will. Although in fairness to your dad, he doesn't know he is an alien.' said Grandad.

He then sighed, 'The world just can't handle anyone or anything that is different.'

'So why did you tell me?' I asked.

'Your different Bella. Your special,' he replied.

'Am I special enough to be able to click my

fingers and change into anything?' I asked grinning.

'I don't know. But it's not a game. It can be dangerous. I only choose to turn myself into things that have fingers, as I need to be able to click my fingers to turn back. Otherwise I could be trapped as the creature for ever,' replied Grandad.

When my dad returned with a policeman, he was surprised to see Grandad.

'I didn't know you were here?' he said questioningly to Grandad.

'I was in the neighbourhood,' Grandad replied.

'In the middle of night?' Dad asked.

'You know I sleep badly. I went for a walk. I then noticed the flashing lights in your street and wondered what was happening. Little did I know they were for you,' said Grandad smiling.

'Well, not exactly for me,' Dad said annoyed.

The policeman coughed to interrupt, 'If you don't mind, where is this alien?' he asked.

Grandad acted surprised and asked, 'What an alien, here?'

Dad looked at me and said, 'Tell them bella, where did the alien go?'

Trying to do my best to look puzzled, I said, 'Sorry Dad, I have no idea what you are talking about, unless you are on about the nightmare I had?'

CHAPTER FIVE

Bella's Birthday

The next day was my eleventh birthday. I had a magnificent breakfast with my mum, dad and grandad.

At the end of the breakfast my grandad gave me a small box wrapped in paper that was covered in stars.

'Happy Birthday Bella,' he said.

I unwrapped my gift. There was a set of keys inside the box.

'Bella, these are the keys to the shop Yummy. When you are old enough it will be yours, and everything in it will be as well,' said Grandad.

Sat a little stunned, my mum interjected before I could thank him, 'I was a little surprised you snuck into Grandad's shop the other day.

'Yummy is your shop Grandad?' I asked.

'No Bella, it is ours,' Grandad replied.

'Where did you get all the things from?' I asked.

'Another planet!' Grandad said smiling and causing us all to laugh. Although my parents didn't realise my Grandad probably wasn't joking.

'I told you that you would soon see why everything belonged to you in Yummy,' said mum.

'So, Why didn't you want me to go into Yummy and see all the alien stuff?' I asked her.

'We were worried you would have nightmares,' said Mum.

'I think you were right about the nightmares,' I said winking at Grandad.

'Your dad and I were also worried you would get caught up in all of your grandad's nonsense ideas about there being aliens and other life forms,' Mum replied.

Grandad then winked at me.

'So what changed your mind?' I asked.

'We can't hide you from everything forever. Plus we trust you will know the difference between truth and fiction,' Mum said.

'Also why did that man think I was stealing?' I asked.

My dad pulled out a fake beard and a pair of glasses, 'That was just me pranking you Bella, you know I can't resist. Plus you deserved it for sneaking in there'.

'I saw you cleaning your car yesterday Mum, and then you arrived to Yummy just after me,' I said.

'Sorry darling, it was your dad's idea to trick you. I was just pretending to start, as soon as you left, I put the bucket and sponge away and ran after you. Your dad then thought it would be funny to get Fred in on it'.

My mum and dad laughed.

What my mum and dad didn't realise was the prank was on them because my dad was an alien, and they had no idea.

Remember, you can't tell anyone I'm half-alien.

The End

The following text is the original draft of 'The Alien Girl' by Holly Soorty, aged seven-years-old

INTRODUCTION

Hello" my name is Bella smith and I will tell you all about me. I have a secret it is that I am half alien well my family does not know that I am half alien. I have to keep my voice down because it is an alien voice.

CHAPTER 1

Alien

When Bella waked home she saw a new shop, it was called yummy I did not know why it was called that, so I stepped inside. When Bella stepped inside, she saw lots of alien stuff she was a bit worried because she wanted to know why there was a man staring at her. The man said are" you an alien. BUT Bella was shaking with fear because she did not know what to say. Just then the man waked off into nowhere. Bella tried to follow but the man who worked at the shop was her mum. Bella was absolutely confused because she saw her mum at home washing the car. She went back home but noticed that it was her neighbour washing their car. As Bella talked to her mum a man came inside, he said "you stole my shop". Bella and her mum said "this is our shop not yours so go away now leave". The man ran off into no were like the other man did Bella was wondering if that is the man she saw at the shop when she asked her mum about the shop she said" Mum do you actually own this shop, Mum said" no I don't own this shop because that man you saw was you dad because we just pranked you. When Bella and her family got home they saw so many sweets Bella thought that it would be another trick from mum and dad she asked them but they both said no. Bella was petrified because she things there is a alien in the house. At night she heard someone eating something. She went down stairs quietly so they did not hear me at all. Bella couldn't see the face at all she just saw a really long noes it was really green and old. Bella went upstairs to go to bed. In the morning she checked if the alien was there again but it wasn't there. Bella was scared again she told her mum and dad to tell them about the alien but her mum and dad did not believe her. So, when it was night, she woke up her mum and dad so they could see the alien.

CHAPTER 2

The Suprise

When her mum and dad came down, they saw the alien but then they called some people over to look and find what the alien is doing so the over people can watch it overnight and doesn't disturb them when there trying to sleep. The next morning the police were outside their front door saying with a microphone please come out side with your hands up right now. Bella's mum and dad came outside not her. The police said " do you have an alien in your house " Bella's mum and dad said" we did have an alien in our house but we don't know where it went. Bella was watching out her front window just then THE ALIEN came to Bella and said " I had a baby come see what it looks like Bella said are Yoder and is your baby, baby Yoder yes, it is. Then her mum and dad came in crying Bella said" why are you crying, her mum and dad said" it's because they said you need to give the alien back to its mum and dad to its family. so please Bella can we Bella said ugh I don't know because the alien took my hand and said that it had a baby called Yoder you no like it is in star wars Wait said mum " we have an baby alien from star light.

CHAPTER 3

Home

Just then dad said " we can't keep a baby from star land cos its mite wants to go back to its mum and dad. THE alien said please take me back to my mum and dad. Bella watched the episode and saw where they had to go, she said to head north but the lived in south so it would take them a couple of days but they will go on the journey. They had to go past the creepy house and get there rocket out of there boot they blasted off into space and saw lots of aliens it was a bit creepy for Bella but then the baby alien said I see my mum and dad. When Bella and mum and dad went into earth, they saw a lot of people clapping and waving they thought that why is there people clapping for them. Bella just realised what they did for helping the alien and that's why they were clapping for Bella and here mum and dad. After all that the alien waved as he said goodbye they want home but then Bella saw a letter on the floor and it said this is for all of you it said inside the letter to Bella and family I want to give this to because you looked after me really good from the alien. Bella was crying with tears because she knew that he was really kind. The next day she asked her mum and dad if she could get a pet. They said to Bella you can get a cat or dog Bella didn't want any of them she wanted a alien. At night she looked up and saw the alien she rescued and hugged it but then it said something and that was I will be here forever. Bella was really Feak out. Just then she heard a really loud bang and did not no where it was coming from. She checked down stairs and saw her mum and dad watching tv but it was a bit different because they were watching the news but they never ever watch the news. They saw Bella and her mum and dad with the alien taking him back to his home and it was amazing. Bella thought of that moment in her bedroom when she was thinking of the alien it was creepy because that was the third time, she heard that voice in her head. Just then she thought it was trying to say happy birthday because it was coming up this year. Bella walked down the stairs and said to her mum and dad "what are we going to do on, my birthday. Mum was thinking she said "we might as well go to Nando's or MacDonald's. Bella answered and said " I want to go Macdonald's please they both said yes and so they did.

CHAPTER 4

Bella's Birthday

The first thing Bella did for her birthday was open her open her present the next thing she did was have her magnificent breakfast then her Granma and grandad came round and got Bella ten present's and in one of them were a phone and the colour of it was sparkly rainbow colour's. And in the third thing was a teddy of the alien she saved a couple of days ago. She said to her Granma '' what shop did you get this from'' she said. The grandma replied and said '' I got it from the alien shop remember looking in there silly. Bella stopped for a moment and thought what is all this alien stuff. The next day she went into the alien shop and saw lots and lots of alien stuff. One of the alien toys said I will find you. She thought this whole thing was a massive trick. A she knows who was doing it. Her mum came with to the yummy shop and saw that man he looked really peculiar and mysterious. When she went to bed at night, she saw a really big spider at the end of her bed it was super scary. It was the end of her birthday and she wasn't feeling so great at all Bella's mum checked her temperature and she wasn't cold at all.

THE END STORY

Author message. I'm so sorry this book has to end but I can tell you a little secret. The secret is Bella figured out who was tricking her and it was the alien because he sent all them messages that tricked her and that was a amazing trick for her and how she figured all them out. Then she was best friends with the alien.

THE END

Printed in Great Britain
by Amazon